S0-AVU-122

To all Readers! Have fun adventuring with Avu! Hoot Hoot! Jessy B

'Round the World

Author: Jessica A. Barnum
Illustrator: Abigail M. Francis

Apprentices: Mrs. Lasher's Class of Kindergartners 2017-2018
Editors: Family & Friends
Publisher: Lulu Press, Inc.

Text copyright © 2019 by Jessica A. Barnum
Illustrations copyright © 2019 by Abigail M. Francis
All rights reserved.

Summary: *'Round the World* is a book about an owl named Alu who wants to build a unicycle and travel around the world. She goes in search of the perfect wheel for her unicycle and has many surprise encounters in nature along the way. Alu's imagination, curiosity and determination remind us that anything is possible when we believe in our ideas.

ISBN #: 978-0-359-67295-0

Printed by Lulu Press, Inc. in the United States of America

Second Edition

Visit our website & blog at:
https://roundtheworldalu.wixsite.com/unicycle

For YOU with love from Alu!

Alu loved reading her book about unicycles.

Her dream was to build a unicycle all by herself.

Perched on her vine swing, Alu looked up at the night sky and saw the moon.

It was big and round. Alu imagined it rolling like a wheel for her unicycle.

Alu wanted to find a big round wheel like the moon so she could ride her unicycle around the world.

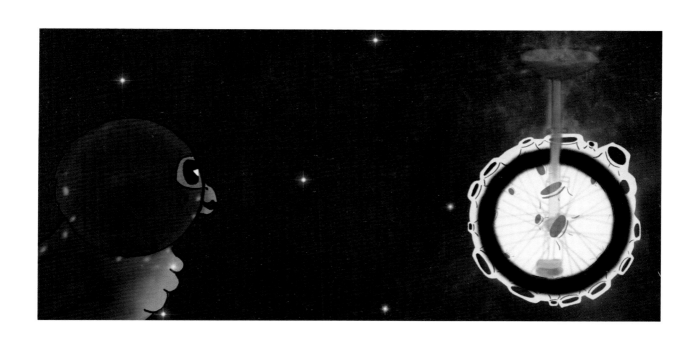

Alu settled her wings and closed her big round yellow owl eyes. She dreamed about her unicycle.

She would search for a wheel when the sun rose the next day.

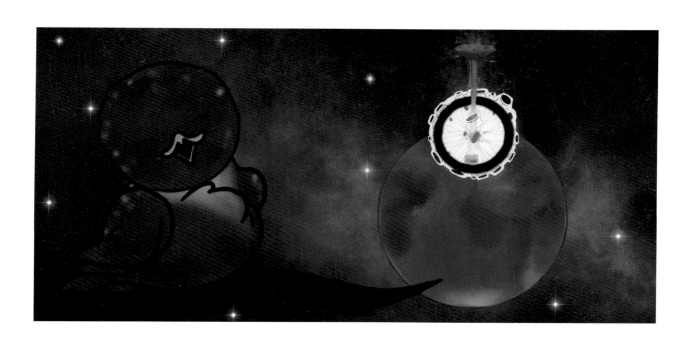

As the sun rose the next morning, Alu flew through the forest and saw a big white wheel glowing in the light.

She reached for the white wheel with the tips of her wings.

When Alu touched the glowing white wheel, it broke apart. Sticky, stringy silk stuck to her feathers.

Alu didn't think a wheel that broke so easily and that made her feathers sticky would roll very well around the world.

Alu fluttered her sticky wings and flew in search of a wheel that didn't break apart or stick to her.

Alu flew through the forest and saw a cave. She looked into the cave.

She saw a big blue wheel glowing in the darkness.

Then the big blue wheel blinked!

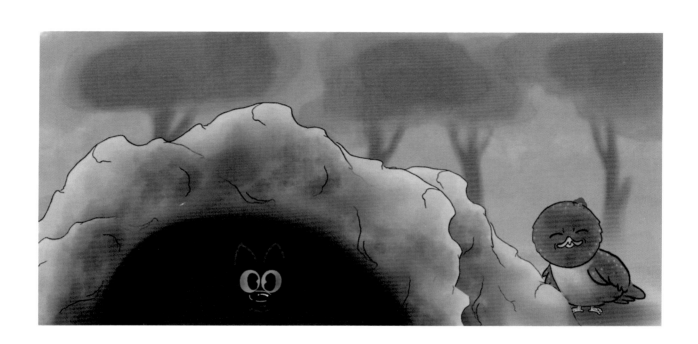

And then a lot of big blue wheels blinked, and loud echoes of yelping, whining and howling filled up the dark cave.

Alu didn't think a wheel that blinked, yelped, whined and howled would roll very well around the world.

Alu fluttered her wings and flew in search of a wheel that didn't blink, yelp, whine or howl.

Alu flew over a beach by the ocean.

She saw a big round green wheel on the sand.

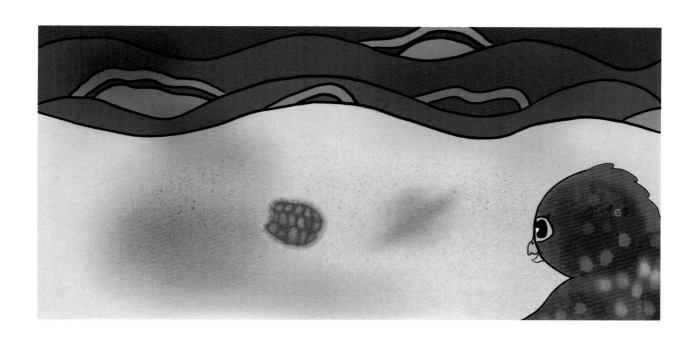

Then four legs and a big head popped out from inside the wheel. And the big round green wheel started walking toward the water.

Alu didn't think a wheel that had legs and a head and walked would roll very well around the world.

Alu kept fluttering her wings and flew in search of a wheel that didn't have legs and a head and didn't walk.

But Alu didn't have to fly too far.

This time she saw a purple wheel floating on the surface of the ocean.

When Alu landed on the floating purple wheel, big long arms reached out of the water and waved at her. Oh my! A wheel that waves!

Alu didn't think a wheel that had big long arms that waved at her would roll very well around the world.

Alu fluttered her wings and flew in search of a wheel that didn't have big long arms that waved at her.

Alu flew over a river and landed on the riverbank.

Her owl eyes could see a big round orange wheel in the water.

The big round orange wheel floated by and shrunk into a tiny fish.

Alu didn't think a wheel that shrunk into a tiny fish would roll very well around the world.

Alu fluttered her wings and flew in search of a wheel that didn't shrink into a tiny fish.

Alu flew over a field.

Her owl eyes could see a spiky brown wheel in the tall grass.

Alu landed with a swoosh beside the spiky brown wheel and it popped open. It sniffed and wiggled and ran away in the tall grass.

Alu didn't think a spiky wheel that popped open, sniffed, wiggled and ran away would roll very well around the world.

Alu fluttered her wings and flew in search of a wheel that didn't pop open, sniff, wiggle and run away.

Alu flew over a meadow full of big red wheels.

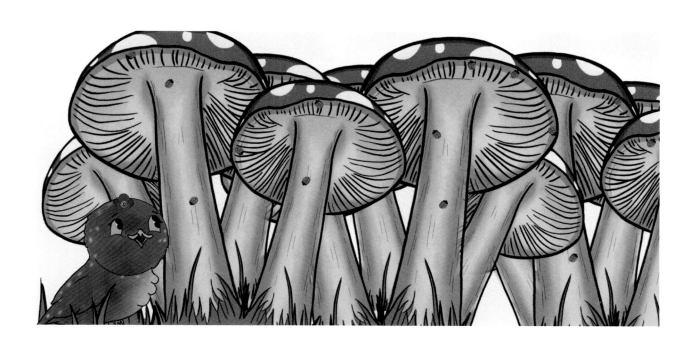

Alu landed on one of the red wheels and it squished. A swarm of ladybugs zoomed around Alu's head. She became dizzy from the zooming ladybugs!

She didn't think she could ride her unicycle around the world with a squishy wheel or with all those zooming ladybugs making her dizzy.

Alu fluttered her wings and flew in search of a wheel that didn't squish.

And she was happy the zooming ladybugs didn't follow her.

Alu flew over a field of big yellow wheels that were swaying in the breeze. It looked like the wheels were waving at her.

Alu swooped down, perched on a yellow wheel, and it drooped to the ground.

When Alu hopped off, the big yellow wheel bounced back up toward the sun to sway once again with the other big yellow wheels.

So Alu flew back up into the sky and perched on another big yellow wheel. It drooped to the ground just like the other one.

And it bounced back up to the sun just like the other one too.

Alu didn't think a wheel that swayed, drooped and bounced would roll very well around the world.

Alu fluttered her wings and flew in search of a wheel that didn't sway, droop and bounce.

Alu flew over a big red barn.

When Alu stopped to rest, she heard a lot of buzzing coming from under the edge of the roof.

Alu flew to see what the buzzing was all about. Then she saw it! A shiny golden wheel buzzing with bees!

Alu flew and tried to grab the shiny golden wheel with her talons. But the swarm of buzzing bees made her dizzy just like the zooming ladybugs. And the shiny golden wheel made her talons drippy and sticky with honey!

Alu didn't think she could ride her unicycle around the world with a drippy, sticky wheel or with all those buzzing bees making her dizzy.

Alu fluttered her wings and flew in search of a wheel that wasn't drippy and sticky with honey.

And she was happy the buzzing bees didn't follow her.

Alu flew over another big green wheel resting on a rock.

Alu tried to lift the green wheel with her beak. But the wheel slowly slipped apart and it wasn't a wheel anymore. It was a scaly stick that hissed at her! As it slithered off the rock and into the forest, that scaly hissing stick stuck out its purple tongue at her. How rude!

Alu didn't think a wheel that slipped apart, turned into a scaly stick, hissed, slithered away and stuck out its tongue at her would roll very well around the world.

Alu fluttered her wings and flew in search of a wheel that didn't slip apart, turn into a scaly stick, hiss, slither away or stick out its tongue.

As the sun set and the moon rose, Alu perched once again on her vine swing.

She rested her wings after a very long day searching for a wheel for her unicycle.

The twinkling of lightning bugs started to fill the night. They made a big round circle that spiraled up into the sky. Alu saw a wheel and her big owl heart thumped.

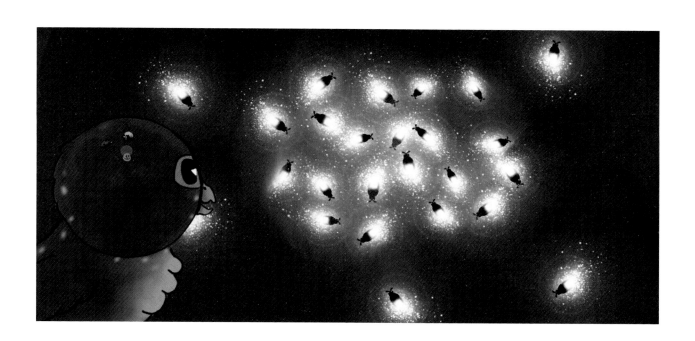

But when Alu fluttered her wings and flew upward next to the big round twinkling wheel, the lightning bugs scattered like shooting stars. Where did the wheel go?

Alu didn't think a wheel that got itself lost would roll very well around the world.

Alu continued to flutter her wings and wanted to fly in search of a wheel that didn't get itself lost.

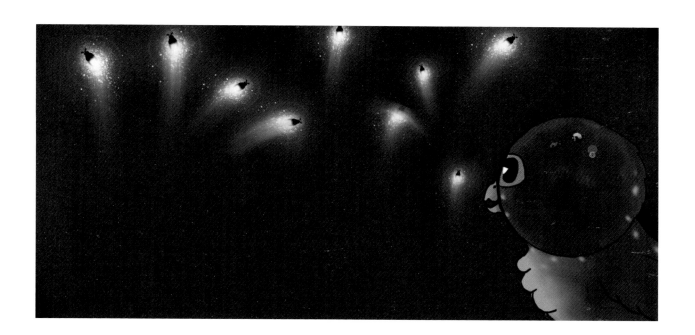

But instead Alu perched on the tippity-top of a tree where she was closer to the moon.

She imagined her unicycle and wondered if she'd ever find a wheel that would roll very well around the world.

She wondered if there was a wheel that didn't break, stick, blink, yelp, whine, howl, have legs and a head, walk, wave, shrink, pop open, sniff, wiggle, run away, squish, sway, droop, bounce, stick, drip, slip apart, turn into a slimy stick, hiss, slither away, stick out its tongue at her and get itself lost!

Just as Alu's eyes started to get sleepy, the twinkling, spiraling wheel appeared again. The wheel was her vine swing that twinkled and spiraled with the lightning bugs. And then a song of sounds swarmed Alu's ears. She heard breaking, sticking, blinking, yelping, whining, howling, walking, waving, shrinking, popping open, sniffing, wiggling, running away, squishing, swaying, drooping, bouncing, sticking, dripping, slipping apart, hissing, slithering, and even the sound of the slimy stick sticking out its tongue at her.

Alu's sleepy eyes popped wide open and she watched her dream come true in the moonlight.

Alu's dream of building a unicycle had come true. But she didn't build a unicycle all by herself. Nature helped her.

The wolf pups howled at the moon and the wind started to blow. Alu's unicycle started to roll with the wind. She spread her wings to help her balance. And the hedgehog spun the sunflower pedals. Alu was going to ride her unicycle around the world.

And her new friends had stuck together. With a little help from the buzzing bees' honey, they were all going to roll around the world with her.

THE END

WHOOOOO is Alu?

Alu is Sanskrit for owl.

Alu is a juvenile (young) Northern Saw-whet owl.

WHOOOOO Knows …?

-What images and facts do you find when you search the Northern Saw-whet owl on the internet?

-When do Northern Saw-whet owls sleep?

-What do Northern Saw-whet owls eat?

-What is your favorite part about Alu's adventure to find a wheel for her unicycle? Why do you like that part?

-What examples of "stick" can you remember from Alu's adventure? How many meanings of the word "stick" can you think of?

-What other things in nature could Alu use to build a unicycle?

-Alu loves to travel around the world. She now has her unicycle. What other ways of transportation could Alu use to travel? What things in nature could she use to help her build those ways of transportation?

-Is there something in nature that Alu could use as a helmet?

About Us!

Jessica A. Barnum is a school teacher. The idea to write a children's book came to her when a barred owl perched itself on a branch outside her bedroom window. Combining her love of reading, writing and bicycling, she wrote *'Round the World* and asked Abigail, her student at the time, if she'd be interested in illustrating the book. And so goes the story of how Alu's imagination came to life!

Abigail M. Francis is an illustration major and printmaking minor in college. She made this project with her teacher Jessica when she was in high school. This project took them a very long time, but they wanted to make sure it was perfect.

Alu is a whimsical and curious owl with a bubbly personality. She loves traveling on her unicycle and hanging out with her friends. But, she does not like when her snake friend sticks out his tongue at her!

Where will Alu and her friends go 'round the world? Whooooo will they meet? Book #2 is coming soon … hoot hoot!